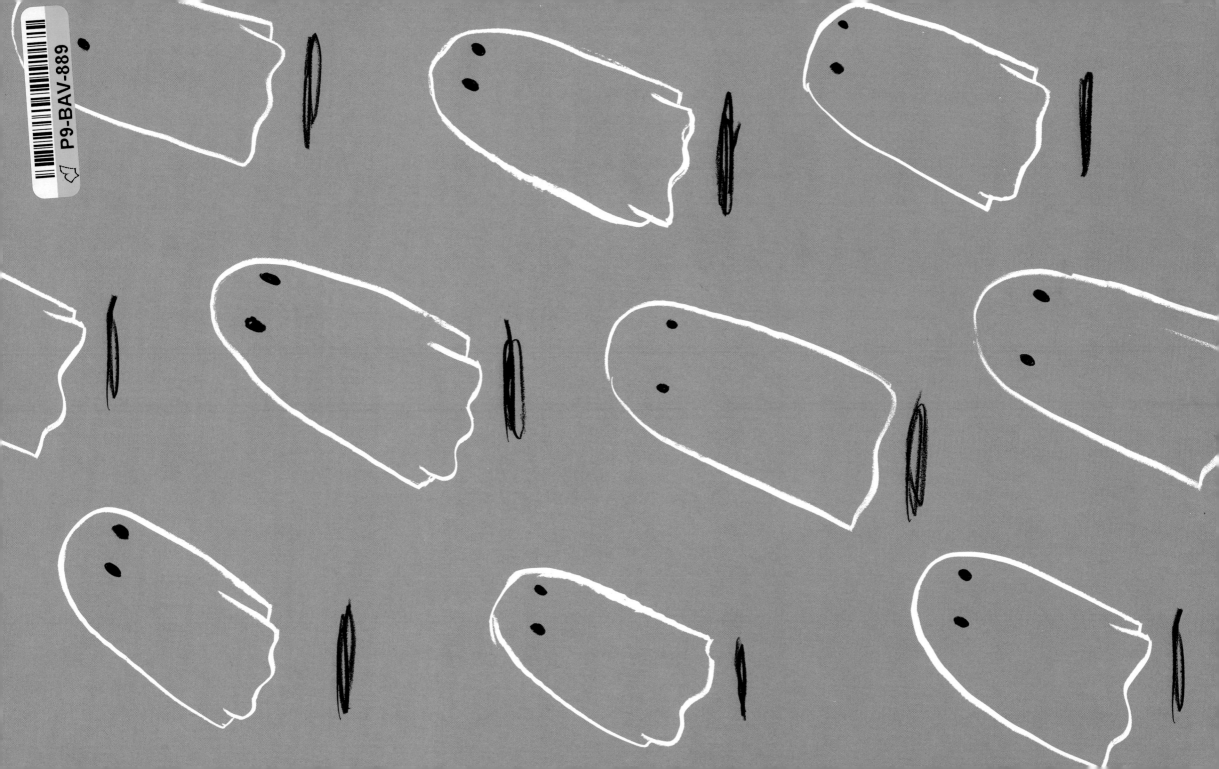

There's a Ghost* in this House

OLIVER JEFFERS

* A fraid of Ghosts**

** The collective noun for a group of Ghosts

But I haven't found one.

I'm not even sure what a ghost looks like.

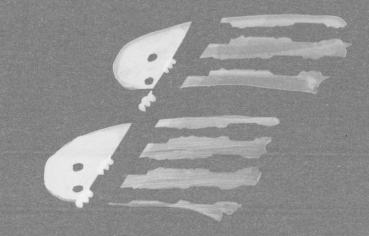

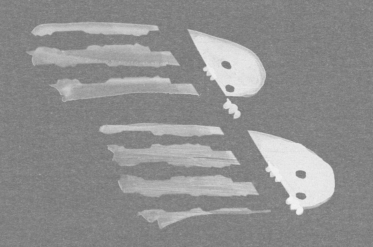

Some say
they are white
with holes
for eyes.

where the lights don't work?

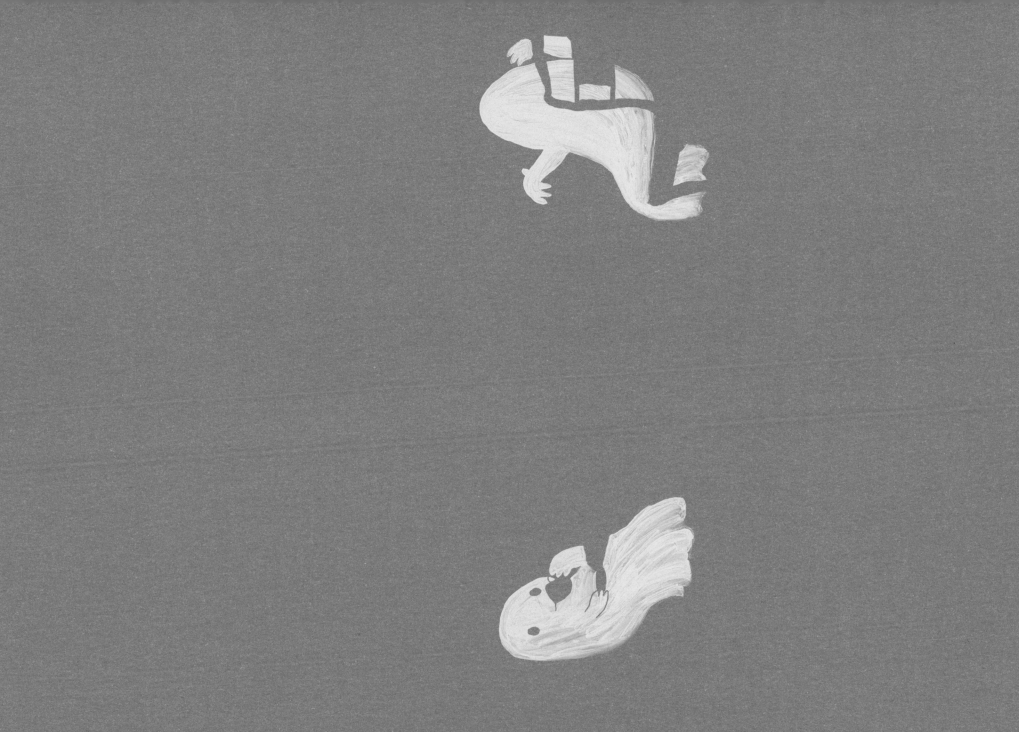

Do they only
come out
at night?

Would you know where to look?

I have searched every room in this house.

IN THE STUDY.

This fireplace achieves dignity with a total absence of carving or ornamentation—an effect that may be just as easily carried out in a less imposing room. The excellence in design of the basket grate is particularly noteworthy.

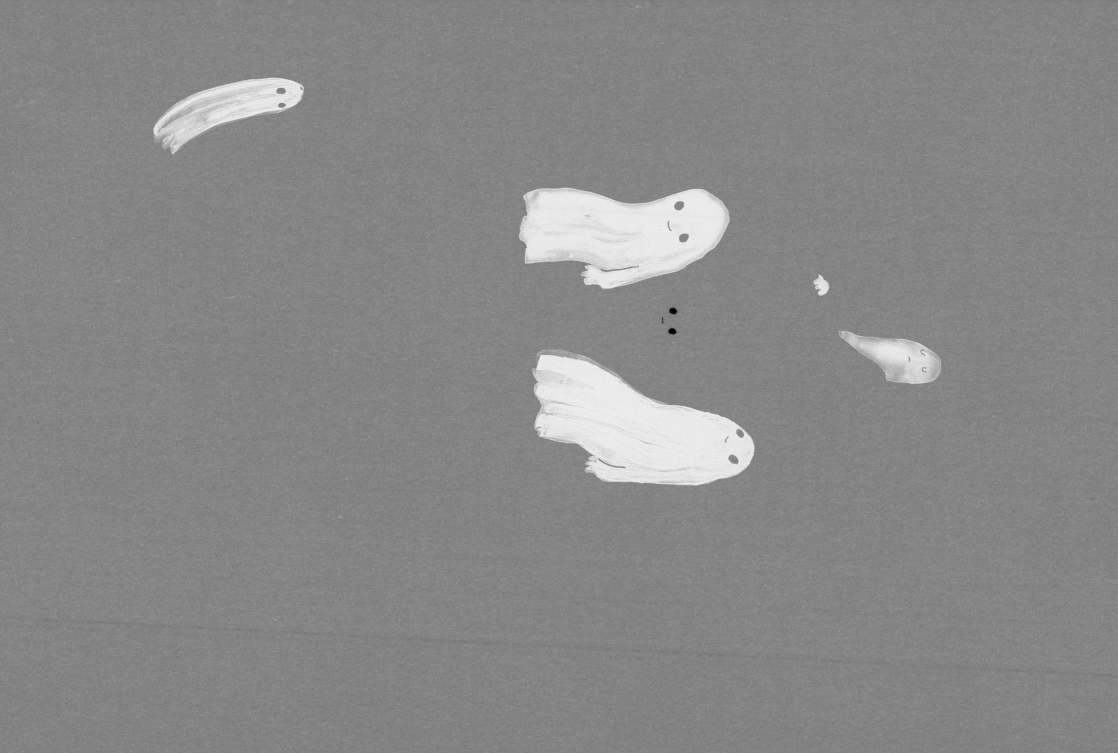

I've even checked
the chimney....

The southeast bedroom contains a fine mahogany wardrobe. Beside it stands a Queen Anne chair.

This attic now serves as a storeroom for old chairs, books, and a covered highboy.

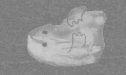

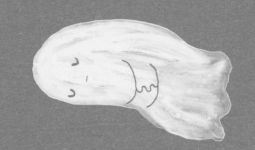

the attic...

behind
all the wardrobes...

and under
the bed…

TWICE!

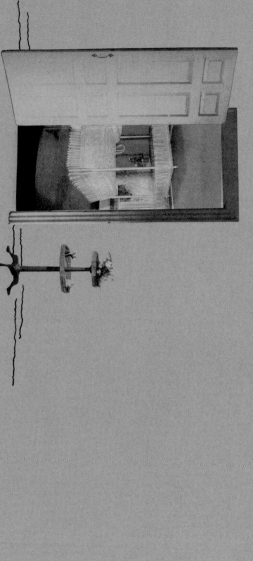

I've lived here a long time

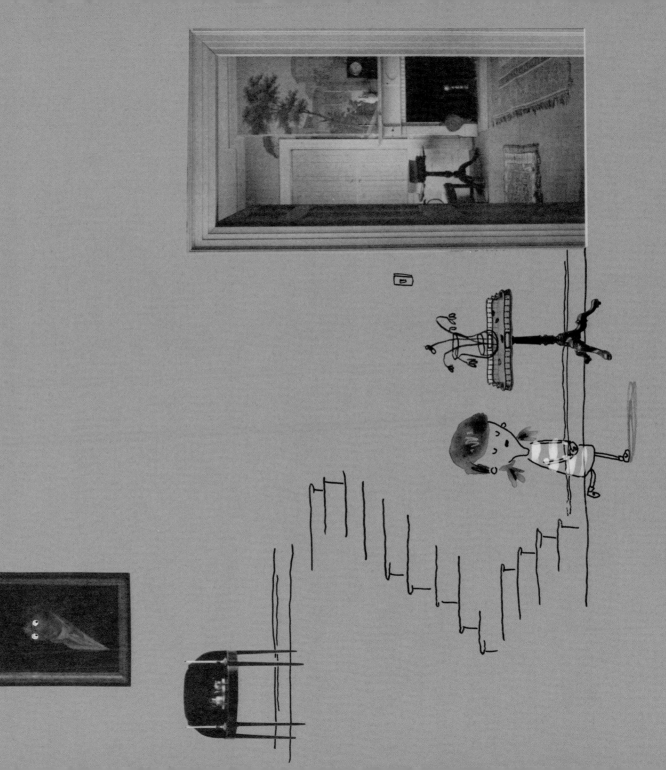

and I've never once seen a ghost.

Perhaps

I never will.

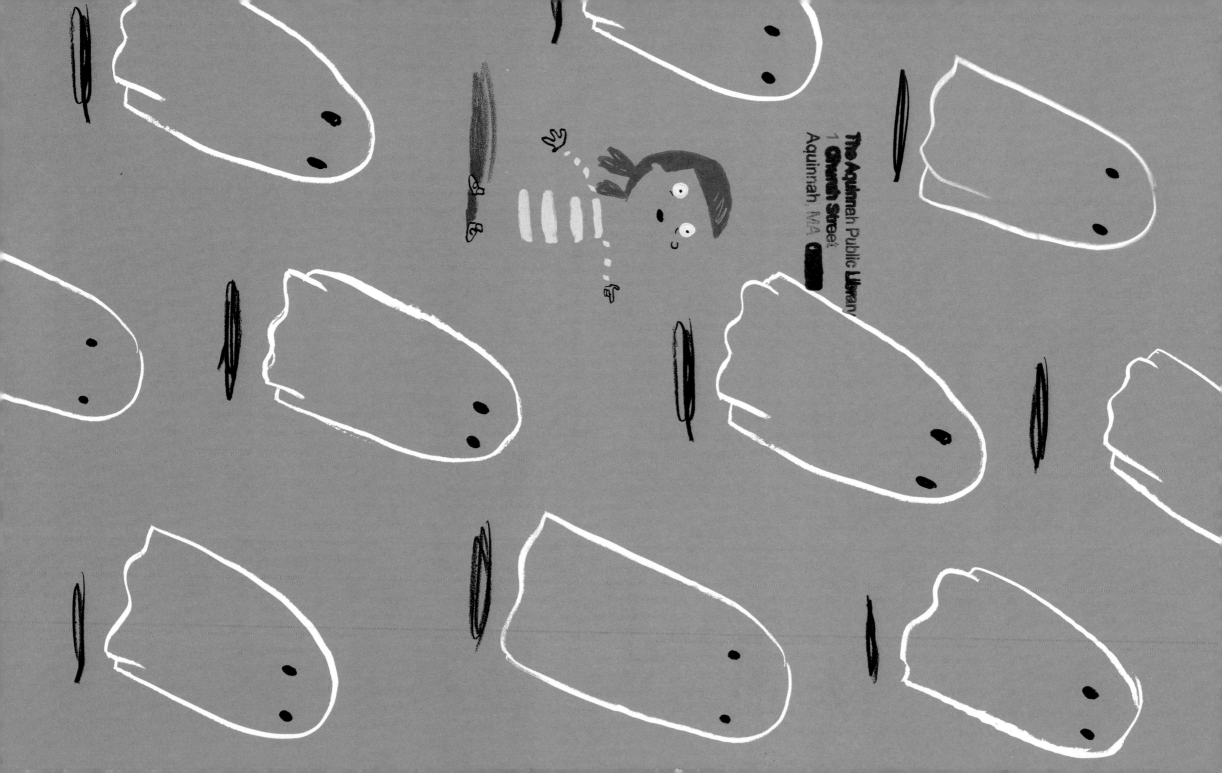